TI-BHS-486

Believing Sophie

Hazel Hutchins

illustrations by Dorothy Donohue

Albert Whitman & Company, Morton Grove, Illinois

Library of Congress Cataloging-in-Publication Data

Hutchins, H.J. (Hazel J.)
Believing Sophie / written by Hazel Hutchins;
illustrated by Dorothy Donohue.
p.   cm.
Summary: When a little girl is unjustly accused of shoplifting,
she bravely tries to prove her innocence.
ISBN 0-8075-0625-7
[1. Honesty—Fiction. 2. Shoplifting—Fiction.]
I. Donohue, Dorothy, ill. II. Title.
PZ7.H96162Be 1995   95-3124
[Fic]—dc20   CIP
                                                       AC

Design by Lucy Smith
The text of this book is set in Lemonade.
The illustrations are rendered in colored pencil and watercolor.

To R.M. and L.H.—lovers of truth and cookies. *H.H.*

In memory of Dickey Lee. *D.D.*

It was Sophie who found the recipe for Monster Cookies. She cut it from a magazine and saved it for the weekend, when she could bake them as a special family treat. They were giant rolled-oat cookies with candy-coated chocolate pieces mixed right in. That Saturday, Sophie herself was put in charge of going to the store and buying the chocolate.

"Could you buy me some cough drops, too, please?" asked her father as he gave Sophie enough money for both.

Sophie folded the bills into a small change purse that wrapped around her wrist. She went outside, climbed on her bike, and rode over to Luca's Grocery Store.

Luca's Grocery stood on the corner of Main
Street and Sixth Avenue. It had wooden floors and
old-fashioned ceiling fans. Sophie liked to go there.
It was always busy in a friendly sort of way.

Busiest of all was Mr. Luca himself—unpacking boxes, filling shelves, helping customers, and checking paperwork—in his white apron with his pencil tucked behind his ear.

Sophie chose the candy in the biggest bag for the best price, and she didn't forget the cough drops. The change filled her small purse. She tucked the receipt in her sock and the cough drops in her belt and held the bag of candy in her left hand. Then Sophie rode happily toward home, except when she turned the corner onto Fourth Street...

...the candy bag slipped from her fingers and into the spokes of the bike. The bike went north, Sophie went south, and 148 candy-coated chocolate pieces scattered across Fourth Street.

Sophie was not hurt. The bike was not hurt. The cough drops were not hurt. The candy-coated chocolate pieces, however, lay all across the road, gently dissolving in the puddles left by last night's rain.

Luckily, Sophie remembered she had bought the biggest bag for the best price. She looked in her change purse. Yes, there was just enough for another bag.

Back to Luca's Grocery she raced—back to the candy section, back to the checkout counters, back out the door. But not quite out the door, because just as she opened it, a lady in a red hat said in a very loud voice,

"That little girl at the door has a pack of cough drops hidden in her belt, and she did not pay for them!"

Everyone in the store turned to look at Sophie. Sophie didn't know what to say. Sophie didn't know what to do. The clerk at the cash register was different from the one who had been there earlier.

"You'll have to come with me and talk to Mr. Luca," said the clerk, stepping from behind the counter. "Shoplifting is not allowed."

She put a hand on Sophie's shoulder and marched her all across the front of the store and down the side to the back room.

In the big back room, surrounded by enormous boxes, Sophie waited for Mr. Luca. She felt very small. And very strange. And she didn't know how she was going to make anyone, let alone Mr. Luca himself, understand that she *had* paid for the cough drops, only not *just now.*

Mr. Luca came into the back room with an empty trolley. He was wearing his white apron, and he had his pencil behind his ear.

He looked at Sophie very seriously. Sophie was very serious herself. She was so serious her heart was pounding and she felt sick to her stomach, but somehow she had to make Mr. Luca understand.

Sophie told the whole story. She told about the cookies and her dad's cold. She told about paying for everything the first time and her bike crash and paying the second time and the lady in the red hat who had said she was stealing but didn't even really know.

It was a long story, but Mr. Luca listened to all of it. By the time Sophie finished, he was sitting on the trolley, looking not so serious at all. In fact, he looked like he was thinking of something very pleasant.

"Cookies with rolled oats and candy-coated chocolate pieces?" he asked Sophie.

Sophie was surprised.

"Would you start out with flour, sugar, and butter—the same as most cookies?" asked Mr. Luca.

Sophie thought about the recipe. She nodded.

"Eggs, baking powder, soda, salt—that sort of thing? Maybe a little vanilla?" asked Mr. Luca.

Sophie nodded some more.

"Cookies with rolled oats and candy-coated chocolate pieces sound very interesting," said Mr. Luca. He stood, picked up some papers, and adjusted the pencil behind his ear.

"Away you go. Your mother will wonder where you've got to," he said to Sophie.

Sophie was too relieved to say anything. She scuttled out of the back room and past the checkout counters and through the front door.

As she was getting on her bike, however, she sighed. She still felt really funny inside. Hurt funny. And queasy funny and sad funny. Mr. Luca had told her she could go, but did he really believe her story? Did the clerks at the checkout counters believe her? Did the lady in the red hat still think she'd been trying to steal? She wished she could prove what had happened.

Then Sophie remembered something. Back into
the store she went. Her heart was pounding
again, but in an excited, hopeful sort of way.
"The receipt for the cough drops," Sophie

called across the store to Mr. Luca. "I just remembered—I have it in *my* sock. Look!" Sophie reached into her sock and pulled out the receipt.

"This really *proves* it," said Sophie. "To everyone."

It took Mr. Luca a moment to understand exactly what Sophie meant. But when he did, he crossed the store grandly, and accepted the receipt.

"Yes, indeed," he said to the clerks in a clear voice that carried all around the store and even to the front door where the lady in the red hat was standing. "The cough drops were paid for on an earlier trip."

He took the pencil from behind his ear and wrote "R. Luca—A-OK" across the receipt.

"Thank you, young lady," he said as he handed the receipt back to Sophie. "I hope you'll be shopping with us again soon."

When Sophie got home she told her mom and dad about what had happened at the store. She was still feeling a little bit funny inside—a little hurt funny, a little queasy funny, a little sad funny. But the feeling settled down as she began to mix the cookies. By the time her mom helped her take the cookies out of the oven, she was feeling much better. And as she ate the first and biggest one, she almost entirely forgot about her experience at Luca's Grocery Store.

But Mr. Luca had not forgotten.

Sophie's Cookies

Cream together:
    1 cup margarine or butter
    1 cup brown sugar
    1 cup white sugar

Mix in:
    2 eggs
    1 teaspoon vanilla
    2 cups white flour
    1 teaspoon soda
    1/2 teaspoon baking powder
    1/2 teaspoon salt

Lastly add:
    2 cups rolled oats
    1 overflowing cup of candy-coated chocolate pieces
        (about 8 ounces or 230 grams)

Stir until well mixed.
    The dough may be crumbly, but if you use your hands it will form easily into balls. For large cookies, the balls should be golf-ball-size or bigger. Smaller cookies are also very good. Set cookie balls on a greased cookie sheet and flatten them gently with your fingers to a nice cookie thickness.
    Bake at the top of the oven at 350 F° for 10 - 12 minutes until a pale golden brown. They are best when cooked through, but not overcooked or hard.
    Makes at least one dozen large, or three dozen small, cookies.
Enjoy.